This book is dedicated to my parents
whom I love so very much —

J. D. and Kay Suttles

Peachtree City, Georgia
May 1, 1996

Dear Ladies,

As you begin this study of the material in *The Excellent Wife*, I want to take a moment to tell you what is on my heart. Before I began writing *The Excellent Wife*, I was unsure if I should even undertake such a project. One day, my husband (Sanford), my pastor (Ed), and my boss at The Atlanta Biblical Counseling Center (Lou), came to me and strongly encouraged me to begin. I rearranged my schedule and began to write realizing that I might end up with a huge manuscript that went nowhere. Early in the project, I prayed and told the Lord, "Whether this book ever gets published or not, I want it and my life to glorify You. You decide."

As you know, *The Excellent Wife* has been published. What you might not know is, God provided a publisher who is very committed to its message — Focus Publishing in Bemidji, Minnesota owned by Stan and Jan Haley. After the book came out, I waited awhile to begin the study guide because I wanted to see if anyone was really going to buy it! Now, by His grace and with the help of Lynn Crotts' and Barb Smith's careful proofreading, the study guide is ready.

I have made this study guide as straightforward and easy to complete as I know how. As you work through this material, please do not lose sight of the purpose of this study which is to glorify God. While anyone can answer the questions, only a humble person can be transformed by the precious truths that are here. Humble yourself before God and cry out to Him to make you the wife that He would have you to be.

My heart's desire and prayer for you is that God will use this book and study guide to bless you and to glorify Himself. I want you to not only live out these principles in your life for His glory, but to also teach this to your daughters and to other women. It is not too late for us to begin to really "be holy as He is holy."

Love,

Martha

Table of Contents

Suggestions for Students:

1. Each lesson corresponds to one chapter in *The Excellent Wife* book except the chapter on "Loving Your Husband" and "Biblical Resources for the Wife's Protection." Those chapters are so long that I have divided them into two lessons each.

2. Read the corresponding chapter in the book first, then go back and answer the questions. Write your answers out in your own words. Take your time and be very clear. Don't just put an answer down, make sure you understand what it means.

3. Pray often throughout the entire study and ask God to show you your sin and to help you to change.

4. Spend extra time and care on the last lesson that will include a list of the areas on which you will need to continue to work.

5. Be careful not to gossip about or slander your husband to the other women who may be in your study group. If you need biblical direction regarding a specific problem that would cast your husband in a bad light, ask your teacher or pastor privately. Then proceed biblically.

Feb 24, 2001

Lesson Number One

Chapter One

The Excellent Wife
Who Can Find?

1. What should be the <u>greatest</u> priority in the Christian Wife's life? See Matthew 6:33. *To seek God first.*

2. What should be her <u>second greatest</u> priority? See Genesis 2:18

   Her husband

3. To what does God compare the worth of the excellent wife? See Proverbs 31:10 *Jewels*

4. List as many traits of the "excellent wife" as you can find from a careful reading of Proverbs 31:10-31. (Hint- there are some traits listed in the illustration of the flower on page 5 of *The Excellent Wife* book.)

   Trustworthy
   does good
   She cooks
   a good buyer
   She sews, plants
   her children praise her
   She helps the poor, generous

   She is not afraid
   make her husband proud
   Strong + caring of others
   She is wise
   a teacher of kindness
   She fears the Lord

Traits of the Excellent Wife Continued:

5. According to II Peter 1:3 (on page 6 in the book), God's "divine power has granted to us <u>everything pertaining to life and godliness</u>, through the true knowledge of <u>Him who called us by His Own glory and excellence.</u>"

Read the paragraph in *The Excellent Wife* book on page 6 that is directly beneath II Peter 1:3. According to the information in that paragraph:

a. What is the wife's responsibility? *To confess her sin to God & get His forgiveness*

b. What problem would keep her from becoming a godly wife?

Not confessing her sin and giving herself to God

6. There are several phrases that describe sin in the first part of the paragraph under the subheading "The Problem of Sin." List the descriptive phrases.

    Sin is lawlessness
    "   " a transgression from God
    "   " failing to trust God + do what He says
    "   " thinking you can get by without His help.

7. According to II Corinthians 5:21, Romans 6:6, and John 8:34 and 36, what is God's remedy for sin?

    If we confess our sins He will forgive us and set us free from them.

8. Who is the helper that God sends Christians to enable them to obey His Word and to submit to His way and His will? See John 14:16-17

    The Holy Spirit of truth.

9. Why is the Christian wife without excuse to succeed in becoming a godly wife? (See page 7 in *The Excellent Wife* book.)

    Because God has provided her in her battle against sin, and when she falls short He will forgive her.

10. At the end of chapter one, you are asked the question, "Are you ready to begin?" to become a godly wife? If so, take some time to thoughtfully write out your prayer below. Pray in faith knowing that if you pray in God's will, He hears you. See I John 5:14

Lesson Number Two

Chapter Two

A Wife's Understanding of God
God's Protective Authority

1. What is your responsibility to God as His creature? (See the second paragraph on page 9 in *The Excellent Wife* book.)

2. List and be prepared to discuss the five biblical principles on "What Wives Need to Know About God" beginning on page 10 in the book. Be sure to include a Scripture reference with each principle.

3.   <u>TRUE OR FALSE</u> (This section is based on the five principles "What Wives Need to Know About Their Works and Themselves" beginning on page 12).

A. God is only concerned with your outward behavior.

B. Wives tend to be more concerned about what their husbands are doing wrong than what they themselves are doing wrong.

C. How you treat your husband could be the occasion for eternal rewards someday in heaven or the occasion for loss of those rewards.

D. It is all right to lie if you are frightened or it would keep your husband out of trouble.

E. The most likely reason a Christian wife may be afraid to do the right thing is she may be afraid that she will not have her way.

F. The Christian wife's focus should be on herself. After all, God helps those who help themselves!

G. The Christian wife cannot help it if she sins on occasion.

H. The Lord Jesus Christ broke the power grip of sin on a person's life through His death on the cross (if they are a Christian).

4.   What are two passages in the New Testament that clearly state that the husband has authority over the wife? Write out the verses.

5. Does the husband ever have <u>absolute</u> authority over his wife? Why or why not?

6. Why does a wife need protection from the influence of the world? Can you think of any personal examples where you have been wrongly influence by the world?

    Personal examples of influence from the world:

7. How do you stand firm against the schemes of the Devil? What does being under your husband's authority have to do with "standing firm?"

8. According to the last paragraph on page 16 in the book, what does II Timothy 2:11-14 <u>not</u> mean? What <u>does</u> it mean?

Lesson Number Three

Chapter Three

A Wife's Understanding of Sin
God's Provision

1. List the four characteristics of sin in Chapter Three of The Excellent
    Wife book. Include a Scripture reference for each one.

2. According to Isaiah 53:5, what did we deserve that "fell upon
    Christ?" See the first paragraph under "Our Provision Through Christ"
    on page 21.

3. What does it mean to be "justified" by God?

4.   What is God's perspective on you and your former sin if you are now a Christian? See the last paragraph on page 22 in *The Excellent Wife*.

5.   Repentance from old sinful habit patterns of thinking and responding usually involves more than just confessing to God. What else is required? For what <u>purpose</u> are you to discipline yourself? See the section entitled "A Process of Diligence" on page 23 in *The Excellent Wife* book.

6.   Explain in your own words the meaning of the Greek word for discipline — *gymnazo.*

7.   Complete the Bible study entitled "The Put-Off and Put-On Dynamic" on page 251 of *The Excellent Wife* book.

Lesson Number Four

Chapter Four

A Wife's Understanding of Relationships
God's Pattern

1. According to John 17:21, what did the Lord Jesus pray and ask the Father regarding future believers' oneness with God?

2. Jesus also prayed that believers would have perfect and complete unity with each other. According to John 17:22-23, what was His purpose in this particular request?

3. What is the Hebrew word for "one?" What does it mean? (See the second full paragraph on page 28 in *The Excellent Wife*.)

4. The same Hebrew word for "one" is used in Deuteronomy 6:4. How is it used there?

5. What is the model of relationships that God intends for believers to follow?

6. On page 29 in the book, read the list that compares "Characteristics of the Trinity" to the "Characteristics of Fallen Man." As you read the "Characteristics of Fallen Man," prayerfully consider the ones of which you are personally guilty. List them here.

    Take time now to pray and confess these sins to God. Plan a time to show these to your husband and ask his forgiveness. (At this time, it would probably be better not to bring up his shortcomings unless he does. Later on, you will be better prepared to confront him with his sin. For now, concentrate on getting the beam out of your own eye. God will help you and give you grace if you humble yourself in this way.)

7. What does God expect from people within relationships? How are they to act? See the last paragraph on page 30.

8. List the questions (in the last paragraph that begins on page 30) that you must <u>stop</u> asking yourself and also those that you should <u>start</u> asking yourself.

9. According to II Corinthians 5:15, for whom are we <u>no longer</u> to live? and for whom <u>are</u> we to live?

10. According to the last paragraph on page 32, how does God want you to communicate with your husband? How might you experience a righteous intimacy with your husband? What should be your motive?

11. What is your prayer?

Lesson Number Five

Chapter Five
A Wife's Understanding of Marriage
God's Purpose

1. According to *The Excellent Wife* book at the bottom of page 33, what is God's goal for the Christian husband and wife in their relationship together?

2. How are oneness in marriage and spiritual growth achieved?

3. If you have not already, take a few moments and pray the following:

   — that your marriage will glorify and please God.
   — that God will show you the sin in your life.
   — name your weaknesses, confess your specific sins of which you are aware, ask God to change your and your husband's weaknesses into strengths.

4. Based on Matthew 7:3-5, what must you do first before pursuing the speck in your husband's eye?

5. List two ways that God shows you your sin. See pages 35 and 36.

6. When someone tells you they believe there is a sin problem in your life, what two ways might you respond?

7. What is meant by the following quote? "Mutual sanctification is the process of helping each other become as much like the Lord Jesus Christ as possible?"

8. According to the last paragraph on page 37, what is <u>your</u> responsibility in the process of progressive sanctification and what is <u>God's</u> responsibility?

9. Carefully review (including looking up each Scripture reference) the chart on pages 38 and 39 entitled "Ways God Helps Us Become More Like Christ."

10. Define a biblical reproof.

11. List the six "Right Ways to Respond to Reproof" from pages 40 and 41. Make up an example and include each of the six steps. For instance, step one: My husband said, "You are speaking to me in a disrespectful tone of voice." I should respond, "You may be right. I will think about what you said and I will get back with you."

12. Based on the Scriptures listed on page 41, what are some benefits of right responses to reproof?

13. Following the guidelines on pages 42 through 44, write out a sample reproof from you to your husband. (Note — you may be tempted to skip over this question: but if you will think it through, you will be much more likely to respond in a godly manner the next time a reproof is appropriate.)

14. TRUE OR FALSE

    A. If your husband loves you he will let "love cover" no matter what you do.

    B. If your husband reproves you in anger, God understands if you lash back at him.

    C. Unless your husband takes the beam out of his eye first, you do not have to listen if he tries to take the speck out of your eye.

    D. When another person reproves you, you may feel badly for a little while; but if you respond in the right way, you will recover fairly quickly.

    E. How well you react and respond to a reproof depends on how humble you are.

Lesson Number Six

Chapter Six

A Wife's Understanding of Her Role

God's Perfect Plan

1. Who was created first, Adam or Eve? Regarding the role of the husband and wife, what is the significance of who was created first?

2. According to I Corinthians 11:7-9, why was woman created? Draw Mr. Hatch's illustration from page 50 of *The Excellent Wife* to illustrate your answer.

3. Within the Trinity, according to John 16:13-14, whom did the Holy Spirit glorify? According to John 17:4, whom did the Lord Jesus glorify?

4. Adam and Eve had perfect harmony in the garden of Eden. What effect did the fall of man have on their relationship?

5. Draw the model "Christ and the Church" that is located on page 54. Be sure to include the two responsibilities of the Church (the wife) to Christ (the husband) and the four responsibilities of Christ (the husband) to the church (the wife).

6. Carefully read Ephesians 5:22-32 and think about the example of Christ and the church to the relationship of husband and wife. Write out, in your own words, your understanding of this passage.

7. Review the "Eighteen Ways a Wife May be the Glory of her Husband" on page 55. Carefully think through each one as to how you might implement it in your life. Write down any ideas that come to mind.

Lesson Number Seven

Chapter Seven

Christ
The Wife's Heart

James 4.13-

1. According to the last paragraph on page 59, how can you determine what or whom you are really worshipping?

2. What does the word "heart" as used in the Bible really mean?
   830 times mentioned in the Bible.

3. If you do not get your way, how might you react if your heart is set on something other than Christ? For the answer see the first full paragraph on page 60.

4. Read the list of common idols on page 60-61. Make your own list of the ones of which you know you are guilty. Take time to pray and confess them to God.

5. According to the paragraph on page 61, why might fear or frustration build up in your heart?

6. In the past, what "false saviors" or unbiblical refuges have you sought to relieve your emotional pain? See the list on page 63.

7. According to the last paragraph on page 64, what does God want from you?

8. According to Allison's story on page 65, what was her problem?

9. Slowly read over the verses listed from Psalm 119 on pages 65-68. Meditate on each one and ask God to give you the same desires.

10. In regard to your husband, what wrong desires have you had? List each one and then make a list of right, God-honoring desires. See pages 68 and 69 for examples.

11. What is <u>your</u> heart set on? What is really important to you? What you have your heart set on will make all the difference in the world in your fulfillment and your joy. Ask God to give you new heart's desires. Then seek after God with the same passion and energy that you are currently expending on idolatrous desires.

Lesson Number Eight

Chapter Eight

Home
The Wife's Domain

1. What is a "worker at home?" See the next to the last paragraph on page 72.

2. According to the third paragraph on page 73, what are sinful motives and what are godly motives if you are thinking of returning to work.

    Sinful motives:

    Godly motives:

3. What should a couple do if they are in debt? See the last paragraph on page 73.

4. What if your husband instructs you to work? Are you to be submissive?

5. What if my husband becomes ill or dies?

6. Carefully read the characteristics of the self-disciplined person in the chart on page 75. For each one of the characteristics, write down some practical actions you can do as a wife to be a self-disciplined person.

   Examples:
   Observe the ant. I could can and freeze food in the summer so that when winter comes, we will have plenty.

7. According to the next to the last paragraph on page 76, what's wrong with being a perfectionist?

8. What "tone" does God want the wife to set in the home?

9. Read Psalm 145:5-10 carefully two or three times. On what are you to meditate? What are men to speak of and you to tell about?

10. Beginning with the last paragraph on page 77 and continuing to the end of this chapter, make a list of what you can do that will result in a godly atmosphere in your home.

Lesson Number Nine

Chapter Nine, Part I

Love
The Wife's Choice

1. What are the three categories of sin that will destroy love? See page 81.

2. Wives are to love their husbands. There are five ways taught in *The Excellent Wife* book on pages 82-84. For each of the following five ways to biblically love your husband, write a brief explanation: agape love, philandros love, "one flesh" love, closest neighbor love, and love as a manifestation of God's grace.

3. What does it mean to **"regard one another as more important than yourself"** and to **"give preference to one another in honor?"** See Philippians 2:3-4 and Romans 12:10. Give two practical examples from your own life of each one.

4. Beginning with the fourth paragraph on page 86 through page 87, there are three unbiblical beliefs about love. Explain why each is unbiblical: love is romance and feelings, love is unconditional, and love is having my needs met.

5. Pages 88-90 list nine common signs of bitterness. When you think of your husband, do you <u>feel</u> hurt? Read over each of the nine signs and write down those with which you know you struggle. In the next lesson, we will learn what to do to overcome bitterness. Meanwhile, realize that if any of these signs are in your life, you are sinning. Take a few moments to pray and confess your sins to God.

6. If you are experiencing problems in your marriage, what percentage of the problems do you believe are your responsibility and what percentage are his responsibility? See page 90 in the book.

7. Where does God want you to begin dealing with your bitterness? See page 91.

Lesson Number Ten

Chapter Nine, Part II

Love
The Wife's Choice

1. When does bitterness begin to grow? See page 92.

2. Whom else might bitterness hurt besides yourself? See the first paragraph on page 93.

3. How do you repent from bitterness? See the first paragraph on page 93.

4. When will bitter feelings begin to improve? Explain. Give at least three Scriptures. See paragraphs 2-4 on page 93.

5. Based on Ephesians 4:31-32, what kind of thoughts are to replace bitter thoughts?

6. Keep a brief log of your bitter thoughts. In other words, each time you feel hurt or resentful, write down your thoughts word for word. Then take the time to go over each thought and convert it to a kind, tender-hearted, or forgiving thought. Use the examples on pages 94-96 as your guide.

7. Why are *trust* and *forgiveness* not the same thing? See the second and third full paragraph on page 97.

8. Explain in your own words the "Two Different Responses to Being Hurt" on page 98.

9. Loving God and others are the two greatest commandments in Scripture. We are told in II Peter 1:7 that we are to be increasing in love. This won't happen automatically. You are responsible to work at it. Begin by listing the fourteen characteristics of love on pages 100-104. Then write down three personal examples of how you can put on love. It may help to review the "Loving Thoughts" list on pages 104-105.

   Example:
   Love is patient. I can show love to my husband as I patiently listen to him tell me about his day at work. I can show love to my husband by waiting patiently for him to meet me at the restaurant.

10. Memorize I Corinthians 13:4-7. Practice it aloud over and over. Learn it so well that you can say it easily. Putting on love is the greatest commandment. Work on it diligently.

   "Love is patient, love is kind, and is not jealous; love does not brag and is not arrogant, does not act unbecomingly; it does not seek its own, is not provoked, does not take into account a wrong suffered, does not rejoice in unrighteousness, but rejoices with the truth; bears all things, believes all things, hope all things, endures all things."

Lesson Number Eleven

Chapter Ten

Respect
The Wife's Reverence

1. Where in the Bible does it say, **"...let the wife see to it that she respect her husband?"**

2. What is the Greek word for "respect" and what does it mean? See Principle # 1 on page 109.

3. Who gives husbands authority over their wives?

4. What does the following statement mean, "Respect is not <u>only</u> an outward show."

5. TRUE OR FALSE

    A. You have to show respect to your husband only if he deserves it.

    B. If you are having trouble showing respect to your husband, you may be thinking too highly of yourself.

    C. If your husband is an unbeliever, God does not expect you to show respect because your husband could not possibly have any spiritual discernment.

    D. If a husband is selfish, it is alright if his wife is irritated.

    E. The husband is probably the best one to hold his wife accountable for her tone of voice as she speaks to him.

6. According to I Peter 3:1-2, what are the primary ways a wife is to go about evangelizing her unsaved husband? See the last paragraph on page 110.

7. Explain the following statement, "Be especially cautious of your words, tone of voice, and countenance as you speak to your husband." See the third paragraph under principle number three.

8. What should you ask your husband to do in order to hold you accountable to be respectful? See the fourth paragraph on page 111.

9. If it is necessary to reprove your husband, how should that reproof be done? See the first paragraph under principle number four on page 112.

10. If your husband has failed in some way, what else is important in addition to a biblical reproof? See page 113.

11. What are some of the possible consequences of being disrespectful to your husband? See principle number five on page 114.

12. Carefully complete the "Respecting Your Husband" self-assessment on pages 115-117.

13. If you have checked any of the self-assessment questions, then you are not being as respectful to your husband as you should. Confess your sin to God and ask your husband's forgiveness. Be specific and clear about what you have done wrong. Ask your husband to hold you accountable to tell you when he perceives you are being disrespectful.

Lesson Number Twelve

Chapter Eleven
Intimacy
The Wife's Response

1. For what purposes did God design sex in marriage? See the last paragraph on page 119 and all of page 120.

2. According to Proverbs 5:18-19, the husband is to be <u>satisfied</u> (sexually) with his wife at all times. What does the word "satisfy" mean?

3. What does "not having authority over their own bodies" mean?

4. How might a wife get more "in the mood" to have sex with her husband? See page 122.

5. Whose responsibility is it to teach the husband how to be a good lover to the wife?

6. Write out a brief summary in your own words of the six biblical principles regarding sex. The principles begin on page 123.

Lesson Number Thirteen

Chapter Twelve
Submission
The Wife's Joy

1. What are the three spheres of authority appointed by God?

2. Give four examples.

3. According to Ephesians 5:15-22, how important is it for you to be submissive to your husband?

4. Why might you fail to see clearly the importance of your biblical submission to your husband?

5. What are some examples of wrong thinking that might help you justify or overlook your own sin? In addition to those listed on page 130 of the book, can you think of additional wrong thoughts <u>you</u> may have thought?

6. TRUE OR FALSE

    A. You cannot be pleasing to God unless your husband is the spiritual leader in the home.

    B. Submission is a "cross you must bear."

    C. As a wife focuses on her God appointed responsibility to biblically submit to her husband, she will likely begin to see her circumstances more clearly and learn how to better deal with her husband's sin in a biblically appropriate way.

7. List, give Scripture references, and explain (in your own words) the four Biblical principles concerning a wife's submission and joy. (The principles begin on page 132.)

    1.

    2.

3.

4.

8. With what attitude should you approach learning about the biblical view of submission? See the last paragraph on page 134.

9. Take a few moments and pray and ask God to help you see the subject of godly submission through His heart and eyes as you study the next three chapters.

Lesson Number Fourteen

Chapter Thirteen
Biblical Submission
Basis of the Wife's Protection

1. What are three wrong views of submission? See page 137.

2. What is the Greek word for "be subject to" and what does it mean?

3. What is the reason God placed you under your husband's authority? Does it mean that you are inferior to your husband?

4. According to the example of the Lord Jesus in Philippians 2:5-8, what should be your attitude regarding the role God has given you? See page 139.

5. According to the last paragraph on page 139, what is the wife's role?

6. The first paragraph on page 140 gives the "scope" of submission. Just how broad is the scope and when should she <u>not</u> be submissive?

7. Give and explain two examples of how a husband might ask his wife to sin.

8. According to the third paragraph on page 143, from whose perspective should a wife be submissive?

9. Make a list of practical ways that a wife might show love to her husband even if she feels afraid of his reaction? See page 144, "Practical Examples of Perfect Love."

10. Take a few moments to think about yourself. Are you anxious because of something your husband has done or might do? If so, write down your "fear-producing thoughts" and the biblical alternative "love-producing thoughts." See pages 145-146 for examples.

11. According to Principle # 3 on page 146, what are some practical actions a wife may do while being submissive to her unbeliever husband?

12. How does a submissive wife honor God's Word? See pages 148-150

13. According to Titus 2:3-5, who should be teaching and encouraging the younger women?

14. Read the list of ways wives are not submissive to their husbands on page 151-153 and check the ones which apply to you.

15. What is your prayer?

Lesson Number Fifteen

Chapter Fourteen, Part I

God's Provision
Resources for the Wife's Protection

1. God has provided at least eight resources in His Word to protect a wife whose husband is sinning. Why would it be foolish not to take full advantage of those resources? (See the second paragraph on page 155.)

2. List the eight resources for the wife's protection.

3. Describe God-honoring responses and give one example. You may use the example in the book on page 156 or make up your own example.

4. God expects for a wife (when her husband is sinning) to fight back. See Resource #2 and explain what it means to "overcome evil with good."

5. Give several examples of practical "blessings" you could give your husband.

6. What does Romans 12:19 say about revenge?

7. According to Proverbs 16:21, what "increases persuasiveness?"

8. Define a "biblical appeal."

9. What should a wife do if (after she appeals) her husband does not change his mind?

10. TRUE OR FALSE

    A. A wife should never give her opinion unless her husband specifically asks for it.

    B. The purpose of the appeal is for the wife to have her way.

    C. Usually an appeal should only be made once.

    D. Using Scripture or referring to God may unnecessarily provoke an unbelieving husband.

    E. Unless her husband is asking her to sin, the wife must assume that her husband's answer is God's will for her at the moment.

11. Make up your own example of a biblical appeal. Be sure to include something like "but whatever you decide, I'll do."

12. What is the purpose of a biblical reproof? See the first paragraph on Resource #4.

13. Explain why it is wrong (based on I Peter 3:3) to tell a wife that she is not <u>ever</u> to reprove her husband.

14. How is a biblical reproof really a loving act?

15. What should a wife do if her husband denies or makes light of his problem? See the section beginning with the last full paragraph on page 163.

16. On what basis may a wife reprove her unbelieving husband?

17. What if her husband scoffs at her reproof or angrily attacks her?

Lesson Number Sixteen

Chapter Fourteen, Part II
God's Provision
Resources for the Wife's Protection

1. One of the provisions God has given to protect a wife is Proverbs 26:4-5. Write out Proverbs 26:4-5

2. Make a list of ways in which a person may act like a fool.

3. Make a list of ways in which a person may respond like a fool.

4. Instead of responding to your husband like a fool would, you must learn to give him the answer he deserves. For the following examples, write out a good, biblical response that gives him "the answer that he deserves."

    A. He in a very mean tone says, "I don't love you. I wish I had never married you."

B. He says in a threatening tone, "If you do not have sex with me as I desire (his desire is sinful), then I will not give you your spending money."

C. He is pouting and giving you the cold shoulder but will not tell you why.

D. He says in an angry tone, "The reason I have to yell at the kids is because you do not discipline them as you should. If you would make them clean up, I would not get upset."

E. He says very angrily and sarcastically, "You think you're always right and everything is my fault."

F. He says in a rage, "I hate you! I am going to divorce you, take the kids away from you, and leave you penniless."

G. He yells and verbally attacks you viciously and you become confused about how to respond.

5. List the seven guidelines for seeking counsel that begin on page 168. Include at least one Scripture reference for each guideline.

6. Based on Matthew 18:15-18, write out a brief explanation of the four steps of church discipline.

7. According to the paragraph under Step Four on page 172, what is the purpose of church discipline?

8. According to Resource #8 on page 172, who are the governing authorities?

9. When should a wife involve the governing authorities?

10. What should a wife think or say if her husband accuses her of not loving him because she called the police?

11. Why is it foolish not to take advantage of all the biblical measures that God has provided for you in His Word?

Lesson Number Seventeen

Chapter Fifteen

Honoring Christ
Key to the Wife's Motivation

1. What's wrong with being motivated primarily by how you feel? See the last paragraph on page 175.

2. What does gratitude to God have to do with being motivated to be submissive to your husband? See Principle #1 on page 176.

3. According to Philippians 2:5-8, what was Christ's attitude towards obedience to the Father? See Principle # 2.

4. How is a wife supposed to bring her beliefs in line with Scripture? See Principle #3.

5. From where does a wife's "true beauty" come? See Principle #4.

6. What does biblical submission have to do with love? See Principles #5 and 6.

7. How can a wife view life through God's sovereignty and goodness? See Principle #7.

8. How might someone's reproof of you help you to be motivated to be more submissive to your husband? See Principle #8

9. Explain how you can biblically "train" yourself to be submissive? See Principle #9.

10. How important is it to be submissive? See Principle #10.

11. Explain the following statement:

    Your husband's reproof of you (using the Word of God) should be viewed as a wonderful gift from God to you. See Principle #12.

12. What does being faithful in the "little things" have to do with being submissive in the "big things?" Give a Scripture reference. See Principle #15.

13. Explain the connection between being submissive to your husband and being a "living sacrifice" for God. See Principle #16.

14. How might righteous suffering motivate you to be submissive? See Principle # 19.

15. What are some of the potential consequences of not being submissive?

Chapter Sixteen

Communication
Control of the Wife's Tongue

1. Why is it important how a wife communicates to her husband? See the second paragraph on page 187.

2. Define the word "heart" as it is used in the Bible. See the first paragraph on page 188.

3. According to Matthew 5:19-20, what comes from the heart?

4. What is the Lord Jesus' standard of holiness?

5. According to the end of the first paragraph on page 188, explain how a person can renew their mind and change their heart.

6. We are accountable to God for our words. See Matthew 12:36-37. Can you think of a time when you spoke to your husband in a careless manner? Take the time to think about and write down what you should have said.

7. How are you to speak to your husband? See Principle # 3 on page 189.

8. Why might it be difficult to speak the truth?

9. What does "speaking the truth" have to do with maturity?

10. List what you are to "put aside" according to Colossians 3:8.

11. Define each one.

12. According to the last paragraph on page 189, how might you avoid using wrong speech? Make up a personal example and write down what you should think and do instead of responding with wrong speech.

13. According to Principle # 5, why is it wrong to judge motives?

14. To what did Solomon liken rash speech? See Proverbs 12:18

15. What might desiring to be in control have to do with speaking rashly? See the last paragraph on page 190.

16. Instead of wounding your husband back, what should you do?

17. What sort of speech is more likely to result in you having your way?

18. What would be the true test of your motive for using "sweetness of speech?"

19. When the Excellent Wife opens her mouth, what comes out? See Proverbs 31:26.

20. How (with God's help) can you purify your speech? See Principle # 9 on page 192.

Lesson Number Nineteen

Chapter Seventeen

Conflict

Quietness of the Wife's Spirit

1. When the Excellent Wife opens her mouth, what comes out? See Proverbs 31:26.

2. According to the second paragraph on page 195, what are three causes of conflict?

3. Where in the Bible does it tell us to "be diligent to preserve the unity of the Spirit in the bond of peace?"

4. List four unbiblical thoughts that hinder conflict solving. For examples see page 196.

5. What are some of the benefits to you of thinking right? See the second paragraph on page 196.

6. Give two examples (from your life if possible) of conflict over (1) differentness, (2) selfishness, and (3) righteousness.

7. Using the "Biblical Thoughts that Enhance Conflict Solving" list on page 196-198 as a guide, write out one or two thoughts you might think that would enhance solving the conflict in a godly manner.

8. Explain briefly the biblical guideline to overcome each of the three kinds of conflict. The answer begins in the third full paragraph on page 198.

9. What four attitudes are necessary to solve conflict without sinning?

10. In your own words, explain what each attitude means and give some practical ways to develop these qualities in your life.

    Humility —

    Gentleness —

Patience —

Forbearance —

Lesson Number Twenty

Chapter Eighteen

The Wife's Anger
Overcoming Impatience

1. Explain the difference between *orge, thumos,* and *parorgismos* anger. See pages 205 and 206.

2. Instead of becoming angry, how should King Saul have responded to the successes David had?

3. What was the outcome of Cain's anger?

4. What do the examples of Saul, Cain, and the Pharisees have in common?

5. The Pharisees became angry at Jesus, so what did they do?

6. Someday God's anger will be completely appeased. If you are a Christian, His anger towards you has already been appeased. How? See Principle # 1 on page 207.

7. How can you know if your anger is righteous? See Principle # 2 on page 207.

8. What should a wife do underline of trying to prod her husband to complete repair work around the house? See the first paragraph on page 208.

9. What does it mean to be "slow to speak?" See Principle # 4 on page 208.

10. What other sins often accompany anger? See Principle # 5 on page 208.

11. With God's help, how might you lay those sins aside?

12. According to Principle # 6, why is it wrong to vent your anger?

13. Summarize in your words the contrast between the man who "Stirs Up Anger" and the man who "Subdues Anger." See the chart on pages 209-210.

14. What is the connection between pride and anger? See Principle # 8 on page 211.

15. Based on II Timothy 3:16, list and explain in your own words the four biblical steps to change your character from angry to gentle. See pages 212-214.

16. Study the chart on page 213-214 carefully. Make your own chart by writing down your angry thoughts and then write out the "Gentle Response Producing Thoughts."

Lesson Number Twenty-One

Chapter Nineteen

The Wife's Fear

Overcoming Anxiety

1. What two Scriptures mention the wife and fear?

2. What sort of circumstances does a wife typically worry about?

3. What do <u>you</u> typically worry about? Write down your thoughts for each of the areas you listed.

4. How might fear keep you from fulfilling your God-given responsibilities? See Principle # 1 on page 216.

5. What other sins often accompany fear?

6. If because of fear, you are tempted to deny the Lord or His Word, what could you remind yourself of and thus be helped? See Principle # 3 on page 217.

7. Look up the following Scriptures regarding solutions to fear and match them with the appropriate statement.

A. Galatians 2:12	1. We can trust God to help us and to keep His Word even when we can't trust man.
B. Psalm 119:52,114,143,165	2. There is a blessing in fearing the Lord.
C. Proverbs 3:21-26	3. The key to overcoming fear is to put on biblical love for God or others.
D. II Timothy 1:7	4. It is more important what God thinks of me than what people think of me.
E. Psalm 112:1	5. People who make wise decisions are more likely to sleep well at night.
F. Psalm 23:4	6. I can have a great peace from God if I will memorize and meditate on God's promises that apply to me.

G. Psalm 56:4	7. Talk to the Lord when you are afraid and He will talk back to you through His Word.
H. Psalm 34:4	8. Reminding yourself of God's <u>power</u> to help you (if you are a Christian) should be greatly comforting to you when you are afraid.
I. 1 John 4:18	9. God will give a humble Christian the grace not to be afraid as they die.

8. Why will God not give you the grace to jump to rash conclusions? See the second paragraph on page 223.

9. What are the three separate instructions to overcome fear that are found within Philippians 4:6-9. Briefly explain each one in your own words.

10. Using the chart on page 225 for examples, write out a <u>biblical</u> thought in contrast to each of the fearful thoughts you listed in question # 3.

Lesson Number Twenty-Two

Chapter Twenty
The Wife's Loneliness
Overcoming a Lack of Oneness

1. Scripture gives several examples of loneliness and its causes. From reading pages 227-229, what do you learn about the <u>cause</u> of loneliness for the following people: Elijah, Jeremiah, Jesus, and Paul.

2. Answer the following questions from the chart on pages 229-231.

    A. What does guilt over sin have to do with loneliness?

B. If sin is a wife's problem, what else might she do, in addition to repenting of her sin, to cure her loneliness?

C. According to "Causes of Loneliness" # 2, why might a husband avoid his wife?

D. How does a person repent of self-love?

E. Why might a wife be afraid to tell her husband what she is really thinking? What should she do about it?

F. What should a wife do if her husband is selfishly withdrawn and private?

G. Explain the possible connection between manipulation and loneliness.

3. When can you know if your desire for intimacy with your husband is unbiblical? See the paragraph on page 231.

4. Answer the following questions from the chart on pages 231-233.

    A. What is an idolatrous desire for intimacy?

    B. What <u>should</u> a wife long for if her husband will not open up to her?

    C. No real-life husband could compete with the imaginary, intimate conversations a wife could fabricate in her mind with another man. Instead of day-dreaming and experiencing increased loneliness, what should a wife do?

    D. According to "Idolatrous Desires" # 3 on page 232, what attitude does the wife need to cultivate to counter her loneliness?

    E. What should a wife do if she feels excessive sorrow because of lack of intimacy with her husband?

F. Instead of feeling resentful if her husband has hurt her, what should she do?

5. From the three paragraphs on page 233, what do you learn about loneliness and self-pity?

6. What does God want to accomplish through your circumstances and what are your responsibilities? See pages 234-235.

Lesson Number Twenty-Three

Chapter Twenty-One
The Wife's Sorrow
Overcoming a Grieving Heart

1. What is godly sorrow like? See the last paragraph on page 238.

2. What causes sinful sorrow? See the second paragraph on page 239.

3. What (in your own words) would be a godly thought instead of the following sinful thoughts. See the chart on pages 239-240 for suggestions.

   A. "This is more than I can stand!"

B. "I hate him!"

C. "He will never hurt me again."

D. "I'm so humiliated. What will others think?"

4. Review the eleven "sinful" and corresponding "godly actions" on pages 241-242.

5. When sorrow fills a Christian wife's heart, what happens to her God-given peace, joy, and love? See page 243.

6. Summarize the "key" to overcoming excessive and sinfully overwhelming sorrow. See the last paragraph on page 243.

7. How does righteous love grow within your heart? See the first paragraph on page 244.

8. What if the wife fights back in a righteous way and her husband still does not respond rightly?

9. How might God avenge your husband's sin and protect you?

10. Give several examples of overcoming evil with good.

11. According to Hebrews 4:16, who will help you if you humbly ask for help?

Lesson Number Twenty-Four

Personal Review

1. Review briefly all the previous lessons. Make a list of the areas in your life on which you know you should continue to work.

2. For each area you have listed, write out a detailed biblical plan of action to help you. Then begin to implement this plan in your life. Be sure to include appropriate Scripture memory and accountability as well as godly thoughts to think.

As you grow in God's grace, you will truly become...

**"An excellent wife, who can find?
For her worth is far above jewels."**

Proverbs 31:10